Cock-A-Doodle-Do! GOOD MORNING to You!

Colleen Beaudoin

Cock-a-doodle-do!

Good morning to you!

Good morning Mr. Rooster,
Mr. Cock-A-Doodle-Do-ster

How do you do sir, today?

What do you have to say?

Mr. Rooster on the wall ....

give a cock-a-doodle call

It's morning time!
It's morning time!

Rise and Shine!
Rise and Shine!

Listen chickens the sun is up!

What do you have to say?

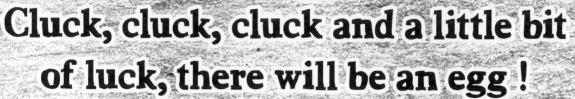

Cluck, cluck, cluck and a little bit
of luck, there will be an egg !

Cluck, cluck, cluck and a little bit of luck, there will be and egg!

Peep! Peep! Peep!
Peep! Peep! Peep!

Baby chicks!

What a happy day!

A gift of love, from God above

We give Him thanks and praise!

Note:

Faith comes from knowing the love our Father in heaven has for us and that He does provide for us every day....

> Now to Him who is able to do exceedingly abundantly above all that we ask or think, according to the power that works in us...

Ephesians 3:20 NKJ

....Luck, then, is for the birds.

WestBow Press books may be ordered through booksellers or by contacting:

WestBow Press
A Division of Thomas Nelson & Zondervan
1663 Liberty Drive
Bloomington, IN 47403
www.westbowpress.com
1 (866) 928-1240

Interior Image Credit: Bonnie F. Goodman

Scripture taken from the New King James Version® Copyright © 1982 by Thomas Nelson. Used by permission. All rights reserved.

ISBN: 978-1-9736-8949-2 (sc)
ISBN: 978-1-9736-8950-8 (e)

Library of Congress Control Number: 2020907788

Print information available on the last page.

WestBow Press rev. date: 10/15/2020

WESTBOW
PRESS®
A DIVISION OF THOMAS NELSON
& ZONDERVAN

Printed in the United States
By Bookmasters